The Thought House of Philippa

The Thought House of Philippa

Suzanne Leblanc

Translated by
Oana Avasilichioaei & Ingrid Pam Dick

BookThug 2015

FIRST ENGLISH EDITION
original text copyright © 2015 La Peuplade
and Suzanne Leblanc
English translation © 2015 Oana Avasilichioaei
and Ingrid Pam Dick
Originally published in French
by La Peuplade, 2010

The production of this book was made possible through the generous
assistance of the Canada Council for the Arts and the Ontario Arts Council.

We acknowledge the financial support of the Government of Canada
through the National Translation Program for Book Publishing for our
translation activities.

 Canada Council Conseil des Arts
for the Arts du Canada

LIBRARY AND ARCHIVES CANADA CATALOGUING IN PUBLICATION

Leblanc, Suzanne, 9 December 1952 –
[Maison à penser de P. English]
  The thought house of Philippa / Suzanne Leblanc ; translated by Oana
Avasilichioaei, Ingrid Pam Dick. – First English edition.

Translation of: La maison à penser de P.
Issued in print and electronic formats.
ISBN 978-1-77166-107-2 (PBK.).—ISBN 978-1-77166-111-9 (HTML)

  I. Avasilichioaei, Oana, translator II. Dick, Ingrid Pam, translator
III. Title. IV. Title: Maison à penser de P. English.

PS8623.E356M3313 2015   C843'.6   C2015-900813-1
                                      C2015-900814-X

PRINTED IN CANADA

for Luc

Chorale I

It was a house of which I knew nothing but the plans and several images. It had been constructed at the beginning of my century, the twentieth, in a city, Vienna, which proved decisive. This was well before I was born, by way of a philosopher whom I read at length, much later. His work had convinced me. I admired his life. The house was simple and austere, and I was rigorous and frank.

Pantry
Ground floor

Chorale II

This house drawn from the philosopher's existence called up another in my own. I had reflected on the first while of the second I had forgotten everything. I linked an intellectual image to an emotive one. The connection was arbitrary. The philosopher's work had convinced me, and I admired his life. The connection was singular. It contained a question and the discipline to traverse it.

East servant's bedroom
Third floor

Chorale III

The house was a method. It was exact and simple. It was austere and obsessive. It issued from a life consecrated to the life of the mind. I cherished a neglected house. It was a house of the mind in which my method lived. I sought its coherence alongside that of the philosopher. His work was convincing, his life admirable. I sought, in the hallways of his house, my method, my mind.

Servant's bedroom
Ground floor

Chorale IV

It was a singular house, and I sought a singular mind. Our encounter was arbitrary and yet coincident. In a sense I was its initiator, and it originated within the limits of my existence. In another sense the philosopher had originated a convincing work and had lived an admirable life. This encounter was at the foundation and at the conclusion of itself. Its artifact was primitive, emergent.

South servant's bedroom
Second floor

Foundation I

One day, a very young child experienced in-difference toward her parents and wanted to leave her family. Being obliged to sojourn there, she developed liminal, perilous and, frankly, psychologically acrobatic postures, in order to occupy the singular position that circumstances had forced on her.

The singularity extended beyond the family: it sufficed to be lodged there for one to feel this. Like a summit on which one had stood or a fold into which one had slid, making it possible to see what was not visible from any-where else, her position demonstrated to P. the extent to which the familial structure was accepted by its inhabitants, how this sketch of human organization also traced a limit whose infraction was only tolerated at the price of disgrace, bitterness, discredit—an unequivocal condemnation at best, a devouring feeling of culpability at worst. It seemed that the thought of this infraction, the idea of a life beyond this limit, was arduous: it sufficed to imagine a situation in which neither father nor mother were identified for one to recognize immediately the unavoidability of missing them. Against this background, hypotheses of afamilial socialist models, novel collectivist structures, radically alternative nourishing sketches were received with repulsion, as if it had been a question of dehumanized states come from a future in which some exponential machination had outmanoeuvred her progenitors. So, no family at all, no humanity at all. From the summit, from the fold of her position, P. contemplated the full extent of her indifference.

Her vision outside the limits thus had to co-habitate with a life between walls. Yet it was equally necessary that she survive in the social territory, one region of which was constituted by her family—a different problem from the first, more formidable because more evasive. At the very least, this was the place where her mind was given back to herself, though within the family enclosure it had constantly been commandeered by the relationship of brute force inherent in all guardianship, albeit for her own good. In other words, neither father nor mother nor any master existed for her any longer, other than formally— none that P. hadn't chosen and before whom she hadn't considered herself, by the same token, an autodidact. It didn't follow from this that the game had been played nor that, prior to this, her hand had been good and her bets, competent. It was even likely that this social game into which her family had transitively propelled her would prove all the more difficult, since she wasn't certain she understood her role, or even whether she had one.

Additional impediments, therefore, these obligatory games where the best bets, those that are strategic and graceful, seem to proceed from real conviction, a consented-to immersion. Consequently, P. imagined a more general game than the one being played out immediately, a more natural role, more profound, of a cosmological scope, which earned her assent and from which she drew the impetus for her movements, actions, postures and even the feints in these human games in which she simultaneously found herself caught.

Entrance hall
Ground floor

Foundation II

Imagining a general game to motivate her role in the human games in which she was caught took priority in P.'s existence. This had a foundational cause, an originating event or, if one prefers, a primary motor, born of a mix of circumstances that, like the chemistry initiating life on a planet, owed the encounter of its congruent parts, the formation of its internal coherence, to chance. It was rather remarkable that this event occurred in the same place as her birth, a short interval later, on a terrain as if prepared to consummate the rupture which the initial detachment had commenced.

For ten days P. was removed from her father and mother, isolated from the family and kept in an unknown, clinical environment. The panic, despair, terror were seismic. Like a plate detaching from a matricial continent, P.'s life separated from that of her family—and she never again took it for granted. God required seven days to create the World, according to the Old Testament. P. required ten to lay the groundwork for her definitive universe. The latter was turned entirely toward Representation, whose figures and relations proliferated, like the minerals, flora, fauna and, after that, humankind in the Biblical universe. A solitude arose, conscious of the external things she absolutely needed and which her representations sought to attain.

As a corollary, an autarchy emerged, establishing a singular regard that could no longer be "deconstituted."

Governess's bedroom
Third floor

Foundation III

Of the ten long days Reality took to arrive at P., the first ones were sunk in an oscillation between waiting and its negation. Despair assumed that acute form in which every minute, every second of every minute, bears a desire lashed by absence. Waiting is a torture that ends up displacing its original motive. Hope soon capsizes, and desire is no longer subject to cruelty. A threshold has been crossed, abandonment has ensued, absence sets in. Something has died whose groaning shadow reappears less and less often. There is an irrepressible sweetness in the certainty of no return, which prefers to conclude with death rather than absence, for which mourning is more alive than waiting, and which will not rest until the pain is at rest. The power that any being possesses over itself refuses both ambiguity and the hold of those creating ambiguity. Something eludes love and is withheld from love and will hardly ever come close to it again, never close enough to surrender to it anew. The old world has foundered. From an isolation, farther away, the new continent emerges, where Things and Nature are allied while Humanity is spurned. It will no longer be possible to belong to Humanity willingly. It shall become essential to distinguish oneself from it, to settle Reality elsewhere.

South nursery
Third floor

Foundation IV

The newly formed land, resulting from a catastrophe and a revelation, would also, and lastingly, be a haunted land. This was due to the particular circumstances of its original detachment—an absence caused by awkwardness, ignorance, and certainly by coolness of love, a lack of essential refinement, wherein—in one supreme human misery—what believes itself to be love and calls itself love is in reality only the often familial pretext for an irresolution, the revenge of a sorrow. Although the absence had not proved to be intentionally cruel, it had occurred in emotional ignorance—a term of pure politeness signifying a real lack of love, not hate but love's simple inexistence expressed somehow by the physical void.

Those absent did not disappear entirely. In certain circumstances, P.'s desire would wander over the plains of her new land, leaving a trace of the figures that did not appear, the arms that did not embrace, the looks that did not reassure during the ten fateful days. On her second-degree terrain, P. raised an abstract army to fight the phantoms. Microworld in her idea-formed world, conscripted battalion issuing from her universe's confinement, it increased the population of representations occupying an ever more extensive place in P.'s life. They proliferated on the soil left virgin by love's eradication; they were the ideational father and mother; they established, on the clear side of ideas, the self-government that would so often be denied by the dark side of feelings.

Southwest nursery
Third floor

Foundation V

It was impossible to know and futile to conjecture what P.'s life would have been like without the inner battlefield. To try to better make out what had ensued for her to, so to speak, extricate herself, to introduce a supposed essence whose circumstantial reorientation would explain all subsequent difficulty along the route, to uphold a universe of possibilities that maintained the pure existence of a point of view: such were some of the (frivolous) reasons for the question. Yet perhaps the question itself, in its material existence, was sufficient—something to constantly play against, a pessimistic and congenital foil.

This battlefield occupied a large part of P.'s life. Many events—inner, emotional, vivid, harsh—arose: aspirations, raptures, fears of the abyss, death wishes. P.'s existence was caught between distress and happiness: their rampant warfare, their steady battles, their eternal tension—the injury of phantoms, the force of armies, the agony of combat (and all love was grounds for combat), deliverance procured through ceasefire, peace experienced outside all connection, phantoms reabsorbed into their own hell. It sometimes happened that the nightly terrors would creep into her daylight hours, and these were the cruellest moments, the eradication of armies by memories increased to monstrous proportions. Yet it also happened that these armies would rise and regroup during the day, then watch over a veritable night, insinuate themselves in P. and instill every courage in her.

West nursery
Third floor

Foundation VI

Through a deep gash in the love of her father and mother, through this breach in the family wall, a direct exchange emerged between the Exterior and P., a field of signification which would compensate for the shaken humanity, the lost love. Thus began a long journey during which Nature, World, Reality would come to life with all the benevolence perceptible to one who nevertheless loves love, a benevolence that P. would reciprocate with a strong sense of curiosity and contemplation. The forests, the ocean, the sky, Nature's overall movement, as in the wind, its snatches, its diatribes, were received by P. as a benediction; Nature spoke, it spoke to her, came to extricate her from her human tension. It wasn't relevant to know whether millions of other individuals were acquainted with this presence, whether they kept it secret, whether its sense could only be private, for when this voice of movement expressed itself, P. felt alone in the world—she had left humanity's noise to enter a state of simple and absolute concentration. An economy was at work here. Each instance of attention paid to Movement put you intimately face to face with the Great World. In this order, there was no overpopulation. It could contain, out of sight, all human solitudes. When you were in it, the question no longer even arose.

Later on, during the brief period when P. believed in the existence of God, she had this feeling of proximity and transparency, the conviction of the direct and agreed-upon connection with Him—a connection beyond the walls of the Church to which, in comparison, she was never bound.

West terrace
Third floor

Foundation VII

Nature, the universe of Things, the Exterior were always the pillars of Reality for P.—a reality free of humanity, where, by contrast, the ensuing activities, rules, interactions and connections had proved to be, from the Ten Days onwards, essentially unstable. As family relationships constitute originating models of human relations, P. became a kind of misanthrope, an "ananthrope," for whom the amiability of the human race, particularly in its numerous collective existences, was nullified by the personal misery harboured by many of its members—or, conversely and in as neutralizing a manner, its most inspired members were suffocated by groups, their breath shortened, their aims narrowed, their methods made rigid. P. never really understood how such relations— almost the whole range of what was generally practiced around her—could be natural, why these relations should be grasped as banal inter- actions into which one slid as though into one's own nature. Even their complexity, which could have whetted the appetite of those intellects most avid for systems, seemed to attract only those wanting one to change or be cured—and also those who, through a dilettantism despised in its practice and adulated in its outcome, elaborated on the inconsistencies at leisure.

P. didn't feel herself to be part of the game, even when the others attempted to include her. Deep down, she maintained a polite strangeness, a permanent doubt, a coldness made less evident by the fact that, on the surface, her relations were tormented and awkward, and generally too emotional. Yet these relations existed precisely due to this coldness, because P. could, in a way, permit herself to have them. They didn't reach the ground of her true self, the one uncovered through absence—this fissure in the familial organicity that had revealed to her, beyond her human crust, the mantle of her living flesh and with it, in her vibrant core, the telluric nucleus of her individuality.

Dining room
Ground floor

Foundation VIII

P. saw in each person, in each encounter, a possible candidate for love—unless their entry into the game was excluded by reasons whose range was as varied as human fauna, a sum of singular properties, a catalogue of idiosyncrasies. The admissible candidates were secretly stared at, scrutinized. Their intentions gave rise to complex, even vertiginous, speculations. The candidates were precious, made of gold, pure treasures, desired in the splendour of their uniqueness, conceived of as entire universes whose apparent distance, disinterest, closure had to include breaches. P. imagined that every breach led to the true, pure and omniscient centre (in regard to each being's own universe) of those she contemplated. She supposed that these beings were in themselves as she was in herself, that all interiorities had a similarly transparent atmosphere, the same variable climate, an allied meteorology. She was convinced that each person possessed the vibrant centre of a desire as fierce as hers or, as she formulated it to herself later, at least so strong that each would not rest until having entered into direct rapport with the others—beyond social domains and before human conventions, animalistic, from heart to heart, from brain to brain, in the purity of the best intentions, in the transparency of a reciprocal will placed above everything, without interference, *sub specie aeternitatis.*

North guest room
Third floor

Foundation IX

Thus, P. never ceased looking for encounters
or prompting events comprised of quasi-secret
intersections (for she insisted on this extremely
abstract thing that a sharp and reciprocal feeling
is, in a sense), these liaisons between two beings
after which they will never leave each other,
because no matter where they are in the world,
no matter the distance that separates them, they
will try to reunite. And once reunited, a door
will await them in the other to which they will
hold the key.

For a very long time, P. did not comprehend
the extreme rarity of these relationships. The
capacity for transparency—the possibility and,
beyond it, the desire to tell everything, to not be
afraid of the other's retreat from what one reveals
of oneself—was neither universally shared nor
even desired or simply understood. In the end,
this kind of human reality was highly improbable

and absent from the commonplaces of work, daily activities and communities. Sometimes, a fiction might describe it, but in such cases, the transparency would appear as a final, dramatic moment, an often painful dénouement at the end of which each one returned to their own aloofness, forgetful of this promontory from which they had just come, indifferent to this entirely other kind of life in which they had emerged, fleetingly since each returned home, pressured by the conventions that rather parsimoniously allowed these excursions in the open air.

East guest room
Third floor

Foundation X

Just as waiting (the excess of waiting) had made P. cross beyond the wall of familial love, while causing her to feel the strange composition of this love—partly emotional, certainly, but also partly institutional—it had likewise made her perceive the circumstantial and practical character of many loves as equivalent to the institutional aspect.

This character could not be blamed on anyone. And yet, its irreproachability constituted precisely the border that P. had crossed during her wait. It was not that the other space that P. had entered formed a moral world—besides, any reproach as such did not come close to being the main issue. It was necessary, rather, to speak of suffering, provoked exactly by what was irreproachable, a suffering which, as much according to norms as to P. but for opposite reasons, should not have occurred, or in any case not in a manner so sharp, so deep.

In fact, this depth constituted the exact measure of what P. called Genuine Love. Yet the line of irreproachability stopped there, just short of this love. In terms of such love, the waiting had revealed a real absence. In terms of what P. called, by contrast, Practical Love, they had come every day, they had observed her sadness from behind glass where they could not be seen by her. This non-reciprocal physical situation had become, so to speak, a physics of separation, distinguishing Genuine Love from Practical Love and establishing two incommunicable world orders. Never would Practical Love accept the reasons of Genuine Love, its vision, its drive. Never would Genuine Love consent to forget itself so as to rejoin the bustling districts of Practical Love—not out of eternal rancour, but out of emotional knowledge, a comprehension not contradicted by the circumstances that followed. But above all, the vitreous pane had placed P. more generally *in vitro*, incubating the idea that to itself the individual was its own artifact.

On the other hand and by the same argument, this glassed-in space propelled her directly into the Great World, beyond the protective membrane of the family, so that she found herself entirely *in vivo*. Here, in this solitary posture where her infinite smallness was alongside an infinite greatness, she had to emit her own representations rather than those modulated by the family enclave. An autonomy was born there which, due to its very concept, no longer allowed its own negation or any other type of disapproval.

North terrace
Third floor

Foundation XI

For this reason, the return to the family enclosure proved to be difficult—though bearable because around the apartment where P.'s parents lived, there were a few stretches of nature in which the Great World could immediately be found. Here, no underlying disquiet ruled, but instead lavish certainty, ease, inspiration. Existence sufficed for things to be that way, and it was so for every mobile and immobile thing. Beyond the division of the kingdoms could be found beings, each in their primordial simplicity, absolutely irreducible with respect to the opinions and needs of their contemporaries. When P. advanced towards the shadow of the poplars, over the hillock stretching near a vibrant marsh, and felt herself one element among the others of the Great World, she conceived of the latter more as a portrait than a population—a mechanism deftly articulated by each of its components. Nothing thrilled her as much as contemplating their coherence, as the idea that each being, autonomous in its existence and a world unto itself, truly wanted to maintain the body that had been made for it, and through that, ally itself with others in order to play the immemorial game from memory. Here, neither reticence nor rupture, nor a card house of attitudes, plans camouflaging other plans, labyrinths of reasons, genealogies of excuses, hierarchically imposed visions, metonymical partialities and afferent condemnations, subsets, sides taken by coteries and their synonyms (gangs, factions, castes, clans, cliques, sects, tribes), Power—powers of all orders except that of being true. Here, the pure dispersal of the world was to be found, inconclusive, offered to curiosity, to its urges and speculations, without ceremony. All this, the thing and the consciousness of the thing, existing for pleasure alone.

East terrace
Ground floor

Foundation XII

For P., human communication was never a given. Each being was perceived as a navigating island, and its solitary condition, combined with the disproportionate greatness of the ocean, the unpredictable routes and various flat refusals, made for scarce encounters. Each contact, and above all each conversation, in particular each conversation that had any life, implied in one way or another permission to enter and perhaps, if there were grounds for further acquaintance, authorization to stay—which generally came down to establishing a rhythm of frequentation where a sort of law of least desire applied that set the number of comings and goings between the territories according to the motives of, let's say, the coldest being.

Other laws were added that further reduced the margin of desire. Just like families, communities were the Olympuses in which one was forced to believe, and these human macroscopes were constituted by thin threads of assent—as thin as the frail existences generating them. Promoted to the rank of genuine entities, they availed themselves of a force equal to the laws of Nature, eventually taking precedence. Their initial assents were concealed to bolster the idea that beings are completely determined, and enveloped in cultures erected as organic powers, outside of which it was deemed puerile and romantic to seek to situate oneself.

P. had never had the feeling of belonging essentially to a community whose reasons she accepted as natural and whose rules she knew by heart and applied in a competent, convincing manner. She felt instead like a heretic in her belief, surprised that no one questioned her presence or her comings and goings, that no one perceived the feeling of strangeness articulating her skilful mimicry—and with it, her state as intruder and the real motive for excommunicating her. Much later, she came to understand that her wanderings were deemed normal, and that this sufficed for her to be treated as a citizen by rights of every community to which she reputedly belonged. Her feeling of detachment, her representation of freedom were considered negligible—as negligible as her more socialized peers' feeling of attachment and their acceptance of being determined.

Living room
Second floor

Foundation XIII

P. bore one and only one terror inside her to
which all the others were reduced, however
dissimilar they appeared at first: the terror that
love would suddenly cease. That the fundamental
affections—the most passionate and thus the
most necessary—those to which one ardently
pledged, even devoted oneself, would lose their
object and heart abruptly, and vanish before
one's loving eyes in a stray moment, full of
all the years which would be simultaneously
excised. Yet the profundity that is in its nature,
this faculty that consists in observing whoever is
most absorbing, in loving their every detail while
reflecting on their reasons and relationships, in
knowing all about the person being studied and
cherished all at once, and in not fearing, to that
end, any impediment or shadow of taboo, this,
this rigorous affection, this austere candour, at
the same time as it combs with the fine tooth
of terror the slightest shudder of a hypothetical

end, only results in getting love knocked up with the spectre of its cessation.

An extreme complication developed in P.'s life in regard to the bonds of love, a complication consisting of ambiguities, vacillations, uncertainties. P. found herself caught amid this throng, solitary beneath their barricade, knowing only that she could cross it if the phrases she sent out like transparent probes into an opaque environment would reach someone whose convictions would make them visible. It was at the age of twenty that P. received an actual response, which determined the forming of a first alliance. In a sense, her encounter with Professor S. would not have been possible if P.'s feeling of solitude hadn't been so sharp or given rise to a vigilance that had invested in a multitude of intersections what no real love had yet demanded of her.

This bond commenced with a question put to Professor S. as he was on his way home one evening—a question that arose in P.'s throat out of nothing, stronger than she, quite audacious, rather eccentric, probably kamikaze, comprehensible only to one who would answer yes. Can we talk absolutely? she asked. It was late, it was cold out. S., for a few moments frozen in thought that reverberated all the way to his limbs, turned around and, with a frank look, agreed. The alliance was formed there, in that moment, forever.

South bedroom
Second floor

Foundation XIV

The concept was born with the thing. For P., every love came from a reciprocal decision to maintain it, as well as from real affection. Thus, affection alone did not suffice. It was too linked to circumstance, too wrapped up in the terms of a temperament, too fragile in its ferment, to be left to itself. Moreover, it had to be declared. Herein lay the profound meaning of the idea of alliance. On the other hand, the modes of this declaration had to be such that it was clear and credible. Since ordinary language was lacking, this supposed a shared language of unambiguous signs. Love therefore became an artifact, a construction, a slow induction with fulgurant crossings, where a pleasure like that of knowledge was practised. Love was a culture rooted in a desire it sought to extrovert rather than to model, and whose principal invention was to make itself indefinitely more complex so as to give rise to love indefinitely.

By contrast, every relationship in which affection was posited first became problematic for P. And naturally, such was the case with family ties. Common, though forgotten, knowledge held that blood ties did not necessarily lead to love, whatever their direction—ascendant, descendent, lateral. The family's crucial role in the socializing process, the responsibility accorded to this cell in the education of feelings, the total absence, in other words, of real alternative solutions rendered still more compulsory these ties that blood had introduced, and made genuine affection—given there was any—or more simply the emotionalism inherent in all human proximity, into a prison nest. In rare cases, affection predominated. Otherwise (and it was almost always otherwise), it was deployed like a field mined with vindications from previous relationships, a pathogenic heritage interfering with the genealogy of the flesh.

P. believed that affections born within the family enclosure had *a fortiori* to be declared, that they demanded a clear awareness of their originating circumstance and a wariness of their surges, and that, in reality, from the moment they became genuine affections, they broke away from the family.

Office
Second floor

Foundation XV

Throughout the twenty years that elapsed before the forming of a first alliance, P. lived alone. After the forming of this alliance, she lived alone differently. She did not fall asleep cradled by thoughts of someone whose love she imagined. She lay down and dozed in the cocoon of the World. Thus, it was not the nights and their dreams that the new bond came to inhabit, but the days. It was there, in waking life, that it made a difference.

Most importantly, this friendship introduced conversations into P.'s universe. In fact, the relationship between P. and Professor S. consisted entirely in what could be considered a single conversation, initiated on the evening of the alliance and pursued through what would amount to thousands of hours—P. and Professor S. eating fine or frugal and often exotic meals together, strolling in cities and in forests and, for the vast majority of time, listening and speaking to each other across the distance of the phone, connected to one another by this cord made for the commerce of language, for its structure and for its flesh (because the eardrum is also tactile), developing out of these long, acoustic sequences the temporal topography, the tectonics of sense, going over them again if the exchange demanded it, and perpetually practising what involved both the solving of problems and the code of wisdom.

This conversational mode exactly suited the idea that P. had formed of the relation to others: something exchanged between two aloofnesses, a barter containing thresholds of proximity, compromise, commitment, free movements where one gives all and demands nothing, slow or hasty retreats, but always crucially the recognition of the other person's exoticism, of their surprising leaps of logic and, all in all, of their absolute prerogative as to their own invention on their own territory. The exchange was made between lord and lord, whatever the other's position in society, for it was always in the absolute that two beings truly met, in such a way that if they allowed the function, standing, or any other position of power, or who knows what standard or measure, to capture their mind or body and filter their part in the exchange, this would be attributed entirely to them. Nothing therefore could unseat them but their own false movements, which they were free to accept without dishonour or to devote some or all of their existence to changing.

East bedroom
Second floor

Foundation XVI

P.'s territory was an unpopulated island in an ocean full of fish beneath a constantly changing sky—so that life never lacked motifs of transcendence. It was when ships appeared on the horizon, or, worse, docked and then returned to the open sea, that P. became prey to her old torments. When her first universe again promised something, when the lost paradise rippled in her memory, P.'s homeostasis in her natural and solitary environment ruptured. A malaise tore the unified fabric of existence, part of the void rose up, and the world's plenitude wore like an aura what seemed stripped from it—its former envelope, its marrow.

For a long time, P. had led her life in the hope of ridding herself of this subterranean void and asserting one day, spontaneously, massively, at the foundation of everything, her natural world (that is to say, herself). There would be, she believed, a rebirth even stronger than her entry into existence, a future state of things in which she would experience catharsis, be rejuvenated, renewed. She would have the solidity of one who was not shaken, one who never despaired to the breaking point.

She understood gradually that it would be nothing like that, that she had, so to speak, lost something, irremediably, like those whose loved ones die early, or whose ancestral home burns, or who are chased forever from their land. It was necessary to accept not that something was gone—because feelings as sharp, rebellions as fierce as on their first day could remain in the heart—but rather that the logic of existence had been changed forever and that, in these other conditions of coherence, through this other type of rigour, the general temperament could live again. A balance of power existed between personal identity and circumstances, one that a true intelligence, namely an intelligence without pride, could make use of, so as to handle what is profoundly at stake—Individuality. In moments of despair, when the void swallowed the day, that was what must be held onto at all costs, that singularity, that bridge cast between one second and the next.

Margaret's sitting room
Ground floor

Foundation XVII

P. felt in herself the concreteness of Individuality, its truth. She knew that beyond any genus, any group, she was one and singular, that her existence and her history stood beyond all generality. She did not understand how someone could be considered an example of any category, could submit to their vague desires for essence or totality, could live by virtue of their *petitio principii*, endeavouring to verify, principally or secondly, prefabricated theories. These paths towards oneself were certainly shorter, but they missed the substance and, from the standpoint of individual reality, in all truth they went nowhere or lead—which came to the same thing—to some groupthink abstraction.

Individuality burned in P. like a primordial fire. She had opposed categories of all orders to such a degree that she had ended up considering her life, if by life one understands existence fused to its own representation, to be articulated by rebellion. Yet nothing around her legitimized this. On the contrary, everything preached reconciliation, this invention of comfort that even spoke through the mouths of Psyche's analysts, and whose sworn goal was to collapse the most solid fortifications erected by those souls obliged to defend themselves against such ancient, obscene conditions. P. couldn't imagine how any lucid being, any integral spirit, could yield to such an extent as to renounce the very fibre that had sustained them and, *ab initio*, had made them. She couldn't imagine how an intelligence that had made its way outside of the Babelian meanders of family relations could then allow this analytical language devoted to their re-establishment to coil around it like the snake in Genesis twisted around the tree of knowledge. And, pressured by the paradoxes of these relations, caught in their vice, could suddenly agree through some inner breach to succumb, to be annihilated. This language, which had foreseen her objections to what it was (resistances, it proclaimed), proved to be as tautological as the familial language. Yet it was precisely this language that, upon contact, had summoned up the same visceral intuition in P., the same primitive revolt, the objection that she would never question without at the same time shaking her sense of reality, her own safeguard. No one could take care of her but herself—neither father nor mother, neither god nor dogma, neither clan nor group, nor an indefinitely practiced method.

P. was not to be reconciled. She refused it because she was better able to endure pain than illusion. Perhaps all of this would never be clear. The familial language and its analytical apparatus were formidable adversaries: veiled looks, indirect remarks, superimposed smiles, innuendos of a knowledge that subtly despises that which it contemplates—infantile and vain attempts to evade the law of the temple, futile oppositions, its officiants declared. They were anathemas to disciplines persuaded by reasonableness and science, better suited to the mystique of blood than to healing and truth. At times, perhaps comforting by the simple virtue of their parsimonious presence—and by the mirages that certain disoriented states produce.

P. would not be reconciled. She was incapable of overcoming this crucial opposition, this breaking of the heart, the fundamental independence on which she had constructed herself. A will to exist lived in this movement, which was its creature. To deny the movement would have meant to doubt the will, break the spirit. Herein a limit was traced, a power was formed.

Kitchen
Basement

Foundation XVIII

The original waiting had created two spaces, one behind the glass, the other in front of it. Behind the glass lay sorrow, detachment and a form of serenity that brings with it a consciousness of its own strength, whatever its originating circumstance, its colour, its tonality, its key. A solitude had been revealed there; the construction of the World originated with it. Representations proliferated in this space—to tell the truth, it contained nothing but these representations, types of lenses through which reality could be seen, tête-à-tête, from the eye to the thing, then to the mind, to its elaborations. Here, clarity was an absolute form of intimacy. Nothing could intervene between P. and the World, loosen their connection, open their symbiotic cell to any category. The attracting force had been created in the place of human kinship, during the parents' short but staggering absence. It had diverted the course of filial affection and had taken on archaic power. P. would no longer belong to anyone, but only to the things of the Great World, and she would no longer revere any love other than that of their perception, their knowledge.

In front of the glass was common life, without tragedy (tragedies invariably led to other places), passing by according to the minutes and hours of the practical order. Seen from here, P.'s considerations were eccentric, illusory. The drama was judged to be impossible in a being so young, whose exacerbated cries, inexhaustible tears, deeply unhappy mien in her overly large crib could signify nothing but her wild state, the disordered expression of a reflexive lack of affection, endowed with the power Nature grants but also with its antidote, oblivion—not amnesia and its pathos, but the simple cessation of sensation, its replacement by some distracting presence. No thought was attributed to P., to her desolate look. No one believed that an emotion enclosed a concept, that a fit of anger or despair was at the same time a genuine act of critique or comprehension, and that there could exist, apart from the contingencies of temperament, some existential autonomy against which the parental powers could do nothing and by which they would be dislodged.

This glass made for seeing without being seen (also for being seen without seeing), and for separating the drama from the contemplation, henceforth belonged to P.'s topography. Transported into her constitution like a battlefield inside a stronghold, it ensured that no loving look entered her without being subject, simultaneously, to a genuine apprehension of its imminent cessation and a practical assurance of its continuity, in a tension felt to the breaking point on the stable foundation of solitude, its certainty, its austere truth. Thus P. sojourned, sometimes on one side of the glass, sometimes on the other. Her memory—the genuine memory that retains the feeling rather than the image of the occasion—failed each time she crossed it.

Throughout her life, her consciousness would migrate between the lightness, the novelty, the smooth simplicity of practical sense—the mode of existence where one feels convinced that one is outside oneself, human among humans, part of them, their laws, their natural mores, reflecting all of this monadologically—and the aridity of doubt, the asceticism in her sense of reality.

From behind the glass, there would still be a supplication toward the necessary and vanished love, the enveloping entity turned stranger, like a goddess who would make you obey, the one you pray to and despise, love and fear, different, oh so different from and stronger than the self, yet the one to defeat from the zenith of one's own individual height, one's monuments, one's statuary, to the most subtle of one's subtleties, the innermost depths of one's guile, the entrails of one's artifacts. Behind the glass, there would be an entire life of the mind in response to the reality located on the other side, a reality engulfing in its institutions' calm faith the response that the despair opposite it, in its stabilized, austere and silenced form, would occupy itself in rebuilding with its own hands.

Library
Ground floor

Phrase I

Once there was a house. The first. Large, full and populated. We were at the table one evening. He amused himself putting entire little cakes in his mouth. I amused myself doing the same. He held them like gems and dropped them into the cavity of his ravenousness. Then smacked his lips in a masterful smile. I stuffed the cakes into my mouth with my whole girlish hand. Thank God for their softness! Cracking up and chewing, behind the barrier of my shaking lips. He was beautiful, big, gentle. He was going to take me on a walk the following day. I loved him and he, me. The meal finished, he got up, went to the sideboard, and stretched out his hand towards a plate of fruit. Then he collapsed. Forever.

Breakfast room
Ground floor

Phrase II

Once there was a house that death shattered. Its former objects were taken away—fleeting furnishings, oh my transplanted forest! Sometimes, I returned to see it. It appeared progressively smaller. It took on the density of inventory. And did not cease emptying itself of him. Only an old woman reigned there, Napoleon rather than Crusoe, still fat off an ancient matriarchy. And who disappeared with the house.

Dining room
Basement

Logic I

In the hospital, I had lost the point of origin of my coordinate system, the originating island coiled in the sea of my abdomen—my navel. It was a point generally occulted, almost independent of the self, whose only function was to refer to the external source that had first made us and whose trace remained in this canonical form for the duration of a body's life. Yet, instead of a navel, I bore a small crevice fringed by a scar. The sign of what had pulled me from the night and cast me into day, of what had formulated, asserted me initially, had vanished. My point of origin was not self-evident. It depended on me, I had to generate it in one way or another. But in so doing, it could no longer truly involve an origin. Instead, it had to indicate a centre, which was a matter of internal organization rather than genealogy. Consequently, it could not be accomplished once and for all in any recollection, any cry, any event laden with maieutic omnipotence.

In short, it could not involve my seeking out a parent to reconnect me, even if by virtue of a merely referential exteriority, to an Exterior in its absolute grandeur. My centre, my principle of order, had to recognize the fundamental fact of the Separation to know, in the first place, that there was an Exterior and, in the second, that nothing from the exterior connected me to the Exterior.

It took me years of constant application to create this centre and build *de novo* the frame of reference that ordinarily comes with an origin. I composed my world as a floating, mobile system whose relation to the Exterior was based first and foremost on knowledge and then on commerce, and which contained a few exceptional connections, unequivocally consensual and through which I was able to humanly survive, since that was my empirical shell. I found it impossible to picture all that exists, particularly myself, as the more or less infinitesimal part of a more or less infinite organism, or even to regard Humanity as an important organ in this great organism on which I could rely, through which I could justify myself—a universe with no exteriority that imminent death and the ends of the century re-establish to save their debtors from nothingness. Although I experienced boundless sympathy for Nature as it lavished me with its breezes and currents, I remained convinced of my absolute contingency, the complete arbitrariness of my situation in general existence. I knew that my initial circumstances had made me a being of representations. I loved these contemplative artifacts through which we indefinitely discuss everything while adjacent to everything, seeking in the span of one life resolutions that flow through the centuries because they are based on a belief in a horizontal genealogy carrying concepts from conversation to conversation, for time immemorial. I gauged that my representational life, coupled with a temperament in which action never had much consequence except in ways of seeing the world, corresponded to my fleeting and transitional reality and demanded of me a position of detachment.

Sewing room
Second floor

Logic II

I lived detached from the Exterior, but the distance was not emotional. On the contrary, the Exterior's character, its greatness and completeness, attracted me with a force similar to that of a great love. I sensed a foundational order that expressed itself still more fundamentally in the most sophisticated imaginings, followed by the most fertile interventions. There was something almost impossible in the proximity of my smallness and the exterior greatness, an immensity in this difference of scale which rendered the juxtaposition sublime each time I thought of it, each moment I saw it through the inventions and other intellectual constructions that, for me, replaced any view caught in the relative obscurity of common sense. I did not feel at all crushed by this extraordinary situation. I understood this state of adjacency as one of the many curiosities of existence, a relation whose terms are equalized by the simple fact of entering into it, while the relationship itself takes on a determinate figure: I was smaller than the Exterior, which was—reading the equation the other way—greater than I, but each of us kept our aloofness in this comparative encounter.

I knew that the idea that I, P., was a being of representations was itself a representation. I knew that the representations, although they were real and belonged to the Great World constituted by the Exterior and myself, gave the Exterior a figure derived from me, P., rather than from itself. A solipsism lay in that, which certainly formed one of the important dimensions of the Separation. However, this solipsism possessed a fulcrum somewhere other than in itself, an opening outside of the universe of representations: my individuality. Its singular point encompassed my completeness. It defined a liminal area extending to the border of my representations, beyond my thought but accessible from it and even, in a certain sense, posited by it. A supposed region, then, but at the same time sensuous. Able to be reconstructed, modelled, theorized but—I experienced this with all the force of the obvious—independent of that. A pure and hard core of existence, an absolute form of being, a unique constant. The point situated outside Representation also remained lodged, for that very reason and by reciprocity, outside Exteriority, equally liminal in this other direction, this other sense. It was a question, then, of the same border, a contiguity where two exteriorities fused: the reality of Representation and the reality of Reality.

Thus, just as the universe of representations constituted my own room to manoeuvre relative to an external universe, a Reality otherwise completely imposed on me, so too did my individuality define a second room to manoeuvre, more vital than the first, relative to an internal universe of Representation which would otherwise have assimilated me entirely into its categories, crushed me in its structures. Individuality made me rejoin the paste of the Great World, its expanse as well as its substance. It made me a point among others in the granularity of what exists. Each such point enjoyed an autarchy, a prerogative whereby one could presume a game of translation between exteriorities, of all that is not oneself for oneself, and of oneself for all that is not oneself, whatever the modes—voluble or silent, prolific or minimal, entailing more or entailing less than the human condition from which, in part, I saw all this. The granularity of existence was so complete that the Great World itself formed one of its points, one of the possible terms of the equations in which I formulated my encounters.

Great hall
Ground floor

Logic III

I felt my individuality all the more since I knew to what extent the qualities that seem essential to understanding oneself and perceiving others could quickly lead to incompatibilities and contradictions, and destabilize the lives of their bearers. Systems of properties proved to be too ill-defined, too poorly mastered, too misunderstood in their representational nature for me to place my body and soul in them as though in a sarcophagus and await my identity. I knew the conjunctions and disjunctions that breed torments, the negations and implications that drag you into their conclusions, subjugate you to their theorems if you unfortunately agree to be the instantiation of a single property supplying the predicate at the core of sentences thus connected. If you considered yourself a member of such and such a set corresponding to such and such an attribute, no matter your ingenious approach to being, your perfect exemplarity, your delinquency, your prodigality, your minimalism, your exhilaration, your angst, your boredom, your idiosyncratically terse manner, you would try to be this and that, or else that and definitely not this, well, certainly that and also this because all this is that, all that is moreover that, and each of them is in fact a sum of what can be known about this—except exceptions which are in fact only themselves. At certain times, the worst, you would have to be either this, which you would fear, or else its opposite, which you would detest; it would be impossible to choose and impossible not to choose, and you would agonize in the arms of a double constraint, between an unbearable life and an undecidable death. You would eventually reply through an arrogant mix of this/that recombined, with porous boundaries, liquid transitions, multiple centres and indefinite layers through which to escape yourself—but always this initial catch, this implied predication, this vertical sentence by which, in the most classic way possible, you would be said to belong to what you would be said to be.

The ineluctability of these systems, their syntax, was thus based on something incredibly powerful and incredibly subtle that lay at the core of almost all sentences, something it was senseless to want to avoid—it would have been, wouldn't it, like trying to live outside the electric fluid. Shouldn't these qualities be accepted as an ancient and exceedingly widespread cultural trait, the framework of a second body from which one cannot distance oneself without backing into an unprotected zone, a perilous terrain outside the dome of civilization, mired in its waste, its ignorance and the forces beyond its control?

I did not fear any of this. I knew that Individuality, in how I took it as detached from the universe of Representation and consequently, from all sentences and their ascribed qualities, was primitive, solid and natural, and that it was precisely this antecedence that allowed me to escape desirable and undesirable qualities, along with their fatal contradictions. Individuality was a third whose reality was neither punctured nor governed by any paradox or property. It constituted the resourceful basis, the continual possibility of generating an alternative that defined my mobility in the universe of representations—some room to manoeuvre that ceaselessly inspired my primitive state of freedom.

Secretary's office
Second floor

Logic IV

I was floating and mobile, detached from the Exterior in a primitive and fundamental sense. This constituted the very condition of my movement to its interior. My motion among beings of all orders was carried out simultaneously in the universes of representations, which formed one register among all the others of the Great World. Because I was human, I had this double perambulation, in the order of things and the order of ideas, granularity of representations gliding in the general granularity. Nothing in all of this was ever fixed, the grains sometimes moved, sometimes moving, too far apart to meet one day and intersecting each day, each hour, at each instant, neurological granules in the head, physiological ones in the heart, anatomical masses, particulate specks, these ones on the side, inside of those ones, following, above, connected, pockets of order in the disorders which are quite subtle orders, themselves pure representations, changing, provisional, like all the beings beyond all the orders, with which they returned as to a primordial paste.

Thought was in this sense something physical. I felt it in the blood pulsing in my arteries, in the subtle tingling of my corporeal layer, in the light but constant breeze particularly audible in winter, deep in the distant forests at nightfall. And just as one never stops except in the midst of some general motion, I only had the impression of fixing my attention on something, of concentrating on an idea, amidst a cerebral coming and going that I could hardly contain beyond a certain vibration. On the other hand, stopping and concentrating did not in themselves lack motion. In reality there was only this—movements among movements, of every scope, on all scales, human or otherwise, representational or otherwise. Thinking consisted in circulating in the Great World, travelling in this discontinuous region that constituted my Exterior, myself, constant and also very abstract, riding on my movements as on many vessels from which to see existence exclusively, so that thinking always brought its own particular consciousness. Myself, pure individuality, I was this unique and distributive point of view lodged in the multiple and moving periphery of a completely granular universe, each of my motions, those of my thought but also those of my atoms, my cells, my organs, my limbs, my entire physicality and all my existence carrying me into a fate of pure transport.

South terrace
Ground floor

Logic V

My movements were prompted by desire. I thought this was so for all that exists. In a sense, my desires were pure representations, without real objects or, in any case, without any exact correspondence to objects that would transubstantiate and fill them. In another sense, they constituted the form of all being, that is, of all movement, which they consequently allowed me to feel. Nothing existed, for an eye, an ear, flesh and human sensuality in general, without the simultaneous existence of its form. Thus, what triggered movement was not a cause but a motif, a figure. Desire was the movement of movement, its geometry, its granular choreography. An aesthetics traversed the Great World, which explained the general and simultaneous connection—novels, ballets, architectures spread throughout the libretto of the Space-Time Continuum. But Aesthetics was also a commitment, a form of lucidity that elaborated the limits expressed in the famous *esse est percipi.* My desire derived from the general physicality particular as much to representations as to what weren't representations. Yet it also stood obverse to Physicality by asserting itself in every being, whether representational or not, so that beings would become intrinsically graspable to me—even giving form to what did not yet exist or what would never exist.

Because desire was a representation, it was part of the life of the mind. Because desire was present in the life of the mind, such a life was emotional. Aesthetics interfered as much with reasoning and theories as it did with sensations and emotions. It preceded the distinction between what is emotional and what is rational, reducing one and the other to certain games of forms. Emotion and Reason took aesthetic channels to spread through the whole of the Great World and convince others of a connection between Individuality and Exteriority—scientific, novelistic, musical, philosophical. In reality, instead of being linked to objects and distributed across Exteriority, these multiple forms constituted the pieces of a complex lens through which I looked outward (in my Exteriority) as I moved through the Great World. Although Aesthetics catalogued the whole of what was able to be known and loved, and therefore of what existed (including the extreme mode of inexistence), my desire never knew these essentially distant objects that it presumed were in its image and in its likeness. At most it could attend to its own lucidity and know that its own forms had their reasons for being within themselves rather than in these mysterious neighbours.

I had to admit that there was something rather than nothing, and that this something came to me through the senses. Yet I considered hypothetical all that went beyond the abstract and physical limit of pure sensibility, all these forms, these figures and their emotional and rational games. I hoped that, at the end of my lucid efforts (if it is true that the end of an existence hastens certain movements of clarification), I would come to a remainder, an intersection between the Great World and myself, a metonymy of Exteriority that would appease my curiosity, on which I would lay my head and fall sleep.

Wine cellar
Basement

Logic VI

I was named Philippa, the one who loves horses. In my name, there was movement in one of its flamboyant forms. I had an ideal of which I expected nothing. I did not seek any being corresponding to this ideal. In one sense, I was its figure, and in another, I would never be it. This figure was the legacy of a lost paradise, the difference between its existence and its disappearance—and its existence had been so extraordinary that this difference seemed inexhaustible. I was this animal and also its rider. I was its spirit and it was mine. I travelled with it throughout human history. I loved those who had loved it. I understood those who had sculpted it, depicted it. It was my pact with, my proximity to, Nature. Nothing judged better than this horse and rider how far to go, what could come back, and the irreducible mysteries.

The horse was also my fleeing, and thus the

fleeing saved me. Inside it, I kept going, in its movement, in Movement. I galloped with the Great World. I was in sync. I entered the Forever—ever there and forever—by this fissure between the universes, between the dead and the living, by this outline of a dead house, emotive and blind. What did it leave in me, so that now nothing measures up to its force, its ardour? So that I search for it Elsewhere, in what diverges, in what baulks, in what the normal course of action fails to make appear? So that throughout my life I approach it via many reconstructed lives—their subtlety beyond any real subtleties, their clarity beneath the root of things? So that I find it only in the written hope of finding it? What exact love and what fulgurant simplicity would convince me to cherish it in having forgotten it?

I was P., the one who loves horses. With the same exact love, with the same simplicity. In their race, I kept going ever earlier to ever later, euphoric and anxious, impatient and certain.

I was their movement saved from the first death. My destination was an appearance. My combat was unreal. In truth, I wanted neither to surrender nor to conquer. There were only the traits of the gallop, to grant me safe-conduct, to make my human enterprise believable and to open certain regions to me, certain borders—of time and space as vast as the race of my desire.

I carried with me in this primordial movement the one whose inexistence contained my house. He died speaking to me. He was dead living in me. I travelled with him. I knew that he loved me. Happiness was inevitable.

Balcony
Third floor

Logic VII

I felt a power in myself simply because I existed. An idiosyncratic and abstract power distributed to the finest grain of the finest granularity. It was not a god or a personified force, nor some universal state. It was neither in the east nor the west, in a fluidity or a territoriality. It was neither a subject nor in a subject. Nor, of course, an object or in an object. It was the other side of my movement and thus of my desire. My origin coincident with my destination. My key. Perhaps, perhaps the force of my will.

Inevitably, Individuality bore the truth of its unique drive, its distinctive summary, which was shown in the way each being approached its own existential force—through the constant detour of qualities and attributes, through the filter of feelings, or more directly, straight on, leaving behind the games of the group or making them depend on something invisible, a way that interfered in theirs and which they called grace. From this point of view, there were dissipations and consecrations, and from a more solitary point of view, distal and proximal lives. The destinies had gravity, the histories, solemnity. Forgettable, of course, in reincarnation and consensuality, in some earthly obedience, some celestial reparation.

A riddle confronted the circumstances, the contingencies. Not from outside, from documentary emotion and the rosaries of proprieties. But from inside, in doing. Not the discussion, but the calculation, the establishment of a perfect and frank language. Measuring and not representing, or rather, regarding representations as measures. It was necessary to avoid the view from outside, its alcohol, its opium. To concentrate. To reach that order in which it is difficult to keep oneself. The life of thought, perhaps, when it is plastic, musical—its scenario behind the genera, the species and their hybrids. The life of thought when it is a dispersive matter, a coherent flesh. And when it knows that on its own terms.

Central heating
Basement

Logic VIII

I sought to know myself, not personally but in my individuality, which I took to be a fundamental condition of existence. To master this limit, to develop it and refine its concept, was to examine the part of the Space-Time Continuum that I occupied, or more intimately, that I was, and by some supposition, some rhetorical hope, to make this examination coincide with a contemplation of the Great World, a sense of its reality. The resolution to this problem might prove to be utopian and the position required to know it was certainly acrobatic. Yet I believed that every science arrived at the problem and its unease. That sooner or later it would be necessary to reconsider all hypotheses vis-à-vis the individual condition. That *in extremis* this would inspire simple and true ideas explaining retrospectively the most baroque constructions and their strange hypotheses—how these architectures, each combined with the intellectual circulation it made possible and which possessed the key to its reality, constituted together one instance of the unique figure of Reality, one region of its extended form. The aesthetic intuition and epistemology linked to the condition of individuality had to be maintained and cultivated at all costs, even if only as a curiosity in the scrapbook of the concept of Reality.

In their mental as in their material versions, my representations, my thoughts were artifacts writing themselves in the sands of the Great World, inserting themselves into its substance, its fabric, and thus infinitesimally modifying its figure. They possessed a malleability corresponding to something equivalent in the Great World, a general Plasticity for which they were made. The correspondence was not vertical, distant like a mirror, positing two orders of reality and thereby creating the thorny question of the intimate mechanisms of their connection. It was horizontal, pertaining to the same order, entering into the same plan that it had come to augment—but this last was extendable to infinity, and so the difference between its actual and its potential degrees of development always remained immense.

I drew the plan, namely the figure of the Great World, as a Reticulum. This concept was itself a second figure, distinctive in inserting itself into the first according to the exact modes whose description it provided, confirming its soundness in this coherent extension. For this reason, the figure of the Reticulum attained a generality not possessed by the figure of the Tree—a vertical model of organizing beings, one that suited classes and hierarchies and introduced between the created orders that mirror-derived distance which numerous theories were trying to reason out. In a reticular plan, it was possible to draw arboreal figures, as well as sequences, matrices and many other forms. But the inverse was all the more false, since all inscription of figures in an arborescence forced hierarchical distances between them that they would not otherwise have. In a reticular plan, the general figure's imposition on the inscribed figures remained minimal. Yet it was always possible to add to a simple horizontal distance the extra organization required by the definition of the vertical link, or of some other relation as complex or eccentric as one wished, in order to translate the relation fully. On the other hand, one could introduce a third thing into any opposition to ease the polarity. Thus, Reticularity was a structure made for Individuality, according a status of singularity to the most universal concepts and figures. In this regard, it had such coherence that the reticular figure formed by the Great World in its totality was itself a singular figure.

Garden

Logic IX

I had lived in a house I no longer remembered,
but which remained inscribed in the Reticulum
of my mind as one of its primordial figures.
Perhaps my head held this form entirely, as if
my body were brought back to the house and
spread throughout all of its rooms on all of
its floors. Possibly I was a homunculus living
in its bedrooms and living rooms, circulating
in its hallways, taking its stairs, its elevator,
accumulating abstract objects and images in its
numerous closets. Possibly all of my investiga-
tions outside the house were yet commanded by
it and led me back to it indefatigably, with a view
to imbuing it with so much richness and austerity,
so much candour and cunning, a mix of the
simple and the complex as subtle as a well-made
head. I wanted this house to be transparent, or
more exactly, knowing myself to be in an opacity
irremediable because it had arrived too early in
my existence, I wanted to construct from opaque

materials an edifice that would transcend them, alloy of a lucid architecture and a pure sense of reality. This, the jewel constructed in the depths of the Cave, would shine from its own fires and serve as a perfect measuring instrument in my movements through the Great World. When at rest, I would be inverted, and it would became my house, my house like the first house, solid and by rights, sleeping alongside the others in the fabric of things.

I no longer remembered what had existed and what had not existed. I began afterwards, and alone. Memory became a science for me. Meticulously, I dismantled the steps that had led me from one thought to another if I lacked the premise at the arrival. I acquired a spatial conception of time. I took from nothingness all that was and all that could be at each instant, and I placed it in a continuous, fixed, eternal landscape where to walk would be to remember or to anticipate. I thought of language as an extended body and the architectured space of its extension as part of its syntax. At the end of a sentence was a room in a house, a copse in a garden, a temple in a desert. Occurrences of the same word lodged at addresses that rendered them unrecognizable. Once again time was captured, laid out, made architectonic. It was multiplied by as many grains as the granularity of the Great World admitted, by as many places as the time scales would count in units for each of their lives. Reality acquired a minimal and light structure. It was a reticular thread where everything could emerge, be linked, be moulded. I lived in it, malleable in its Plasticity. I moved in it, in its luxuriance, its suppleness. I reconstructed it with perseverance according to the plans of my former house, whose figure expanded indefinitely.

Vestibule
Ground floor

Chorale V

It was an abstract house, a construction of the mind. I ordered my recollections there through an ancient method of memory. My language sought its utterance. My will was oratorical. I would not be less abstract than the discourse of the philosopher whose work had convinced me, whose life I admired. I would not be less constructed than this memorization of my singular voice, where I had chosen to lodge.

West maid's room
Second floor

Chorale VI

The house belonged to the philosopher's work, which had convinced me, and to his life, which I admired. It served as a device of displacement from a treatise to an investigation, from a renunciation to a return. There, I passed as through an airlock between a silenced reflection and an integral thought. I rode its force of propulsion between what I had not expected and what, in its being, burned me.

North servant's bedroom
Third floor

Chorale VII

The house opened page by page. I wrote through each of its doors to each of its floors. I circulated in its syntax beyond the modelled words, the sculpted sentences. I distributed my thought throughout the house, hybridized it to the foreign shape. Henceforth, its spatiality was added to my language. I reflected by way of the philosopher's house—which belonged with the convincing work, the admirable life.

Southwest servant's bedroom
Second floor

Chorale VIII

The house lived in a populated area. I would circulate in other buildings. I would know other architectures. I would approach novel urban clusters and other kinds of groupings. They would be allied to his language games. They would border his convincing work and his admirable life. They would spread out from what prefigured them, like new neighbourhoods along the edge of the old city core.

Servants' hall
Basement

Suzanne Leblanc holds two PhD degrees, in philosophy (1983) and in visual arts (2004), and has been teaching since 2003 at the School of Visual Arts at the University of Laval (Quebec City). She has exhibited multimedia installations in Quebec and has published theoretical works in Germany, France, Switzerland and Canada. Her research and creative work deal with philosophical forms inherent in artistic disciplines. She is currently leading a research-creation group on artistic strategies for the spatialization of knowledge. *La maison à penser de P.* (2010) is her first novel.

Oana Avasilichioaei has translated several Romanian and Quebecois French writers, including Nichita Stănescu, Louise Cotnoir, Bertrand Laverdure and Daniel Canty; her most recent book of poetry *Limbinal* (2015) includes translations of Paul Celan. Ingrid Pam Dick (aka Gregoire Pam Dick, Mina Pam Dick et al.) is the author of *Metaphysical Licks* (2014) and *Delinquent* (2009); she has an MA in philosophy and an MFA in painting.

Sections of this book were previously published in *Aufgabe*, Brooklyn, 2013.

Colophon

Manufactured as the first English edition of *The Thought House of Philippa* in the spring of 2015 by BookThug.

Distributed in Canada by the Literary Press Group: www.lpg.ca
Distributed in the US by Small Press Distribution: www.spdbooks.org

Shop online at www.bookthug.ca

BOOK
PRODUCTION
WAR ECONOMY
STANDARD

Type + design by Jay MillAr
Copy edited by Ruth Zuchter